VALENTINES AND MURDER

THE DARLING DELI SERIES, BOOK 30

PATTI BENNING

SUMMER PRESCOTT BOOKS PUBLISHING

CHAPTER ONE

Moira Darling readjusted her pillow, shifting to get more comfortable on the couch. She was halfway through the second to last chapter of the last book in her favorite mystery series, and could hardly take her eyes off the page. There was a whole list of things that she had meant to get done that day, but it had all flown out the window when she'd decided to take a short break from housework and treat herself to a few pages. Now, hours later, the vacuum cleaner was still sitting in the middle of the living room, and her book was almost at its end.

A cold nose pressed against her cheek. She reached

out a hand to pet Maverick, her German shepherd, but he was already gone. She looked up, realizing that she hadn't put the dogs out since late morning. Reluctantly, she marked her place and put the book down. The words on the page weren't going anywhere; they would just have to wait until the dogs came back in.

She opened the door in the mudroom and let the two of them into the backyard, then retreated to the kitchen where she began to make a fresh pot of coffee. She had skipped the cleaning earlier, but she still wanted to get it done tonight. With Darrin, the deli's manager, out of town for a week and a half, things were about to get busy at work, and she knew she wouldn't feel like picking up the broom after spending twelve hours on her feet in the kitchen at Darling's DELIcious Delights.

As the coffee maker began to gurgle, she opened the back door and let the dogs into the mudroom. She scratched Keeva, their Irish wolfhound, behind the ears, then slipped through the baby gate that she had installed between the mudroom and the kitchen. They could wait in there while the snow melted from their paws, instead of dripping all over the wood floors.

She poured herself a cup of coffee, added a dollop of creamer and a spoonful of sugar, and was about to go into the living room to fetch her book when the dogs started barking. Glancing at the clock, she frowned. It was too early for David to be home; he was supposed to stop and pick up dinner on his way back from the office in Lake Marion. She hadn't expected him for at least another hour, which would have given her just enough time to finish her book and get started on the cleaning she had put off.

While she was in the middle of wondering who or what the dogs were barking at, she heard the familiar sound of her husband unlocking the door. Frowning, she put the coffee down and walked down the hall, wondering if something had gone poorly at his meeting. David was trying to find a business partner, someone who would take over most of the cases that came across his desk while he focused on the microbrewery he had opened the year before. She hoped that this last prospect hadn't fallen through. He had been searching for almost a month, but no one had been the perfect fit yet, and she knew he was beginning to get frustrated.

The door opened, and he saw her standing in the hallway. "I think I need a new key," he said. "Mine keeps sticking."

"Is everything all right?" she asked. His hands were empty, besides the keys, which meant that he hadn't stopped to get food.

"Yes." He grinned at her. Although she was still puzzled, her worry was melting away. "It went wonderfully, Moira. I think this guy will be the perfect fit. He has a lot of experience, he's likable, and he has great references. He's coming in tomorrow so we can talk more, but I already gave him the file for the first case he'll be working on. We agreed on a two-week trial period to make sure we get along and that he's the right fit."

"Oh, David, that's wonderful," Moira said, throwing her arms around him. "I'm so happy you finally found someone that you'll be able to work with."

"Well, it's a step. We'll see how the trial period goes."

He kissed her, then moved her gently away so he could come the rest of the way inside and shut the door. Moira remembered that the dogs were still locked in behind the gate to the mudroom, and returned to the kitchen to release them so they could greet David.

"Did you forget to pick up something for dinner?" she called out. "We might have something I can make here. We should celebrate."

.   .   .

She followed the dogs back down the hall to find David still standing on the welcome mat, wearing his boots and coat. "I didn't forget; I thought you might want to go out. Like you said, we should celebrate, and it's been a while since we've been to the Grill."

Moira smiled. The Redwood Grill was owned and run by one of her best friends, Denise Donovan. It was her favorite place to eat, other than her own deli, of course. David was right; it *had* been a while since they had eaten there; between his schedule, with him running two businesses and working on cases, and hers, they hadn't had much time to go out together since Christmas.

"That sounds like a perfect idea," she said. "I'll go throw something a little bit nicer on, then let's get out of here." Her book would have to wait.

It was a Sunday night, and even though the Grill wasn't at its busiest, there was a comfortable hum of conversation when Moira and David walked in the front door half an hour later. The hostess greeted her by name, and offered to show them to their favorite table near the kitchen.

"Tell me the truth," Moira said as they walked. "Does Denise — Ms. Donovan — keep this table reserved just in case we decide to stop by?"

The hostess gave her a small smile. "It's the last one we're supposed to fill, so it's usually empty unless we're completely booked on reservations. She says she likes to be able to pop out of the kitchen to see her friends when they stop in."

Moira smiled back at her, feeling a little bit guilty that they hadn't been coming in as much recently. She and David used to have a weekly date night at the restaurant, but had gotten out of that habit. Hopefully now that he wouldn't be juggling two full-time jobs, they would have more time together. She tightened her grip on her husband's arm. It was easy to get sucked into work and forget that making time for family and friends was just as important.

. . .

"You know," David said as they sat down, "Valentine's Day is coming up. I was thinking we should do something special."

"Like what?" Moira asked, reaching for the wine menu.

"We could go away for a couple of days," he suggested. "We've both been so busy lately, it would be nice to have a mini-vacation. We'd find someone to watch the animals, and wouldn't have any responsibilities at all. It would be nice."

The deli owner looked up from the wines. "You want to go on a trip? I wish you had brought it up sooner. I'd love to, but Darrin's out of town, remember? He won't be coming back until after Valentine's day, and Jenny and Cameron have already asked for that evening off." She lowered her voice. "Don't tell anyone, but I think he's going to propose to her."

. . .

"Well, I definitely don't want to mess that up for them," her husband said. "I forgot that Darrin was going to be gone. That puts it down to just you and Allison working there on Valentine's Day, doesn't it?"

"Yes. I could see if she'd be all right working alone that evening, but it might be busy, so I don't know if it would work out."

"How about that weekend?" he asked. "We could just do our normal date night on the day itself, then go out of town the weekend after."

"I think I could make that work," she said, grinning. "Where do you want to go?"

He chuckled. "I really haven't planned that far ahead. What do you think?"

"Let's look online when we get back home," she said, smiling at him. "We'll find the perfect place together.

We have a lot to celebrate, especially now that you've found a business partner. This is the start of a whole new chapter in your life."

He covered her hand with his. "It's the start of a new chapter for both of us."

CHAPTER TWO

Moira had never been an early riser, but running a restaurant that opened at seven in the morning meant that she had to make the occasional sacrifice. When her alarm went off at five-thirty the next morning, the sun was still nestled below the horizon. She reached over and turned it off. Beside her, David shifted, but didn't wake. She slipped out of bed, whispering at the dogs to be quiet, and felt around for her slippers.

Downstairs, she turned on the kitchen light and let the dogs outside. She fought back a yawn as she made coffee, then went into the living room to grab her book. She wouldn't have time to read it before work, but with luck, it would be a slow day and she could finish it while she was sitting at the register.

She was still half asleep as she got dressed and ready for work. She poured her coffee into a thermos to drink on the road, then left the house after a quiet goodbye to the dogs. Her husband wasn't a morning person either, so on early mornings like these she did what she could to make sure he was able to sleep in. He would be up in a few hours to let the dogs out again and feed them breakfast before heading out to Lake Marion, where he would meet with his new business partner. *I hope everything goes well*, she thought. *We need to invite the man over to dinner sometime; I want to meet him too.*

She was about to turn into the deli's parking lot twenty minutes later when she saw something that shocked her so much that she drove right past the building she had worked in almost every day for years. The storefront next to the deli, which had been empty for months, had a brand-new sign over the door, and the front windows were glowing with light. Still gawking, she turned at the end of the block and looped around, parking in the deli's lot and turning her car off in a hurry.

Even though time was tight, and the deli was supposed to open in half an hour, she hurried across the snowy grass to the neighboring building, eager to see what sort of neighbors she had. She had known that the building had sold shortly after Christmas, but hadn't seen anyone coming and going since. *They must have done all of this work this past weekend*, she thought.

As she approached the building, she looked up at the sign. It read, *Perfect Paws*, with a trail of paw prints underlining the name. She was intrigued; she had been expecting another restaurant of some sort, or maybe a clothing shop. A pet store would be a very welcome addition to Maple Creek. It would be nice to be able to go right next door after work to grab dog food, instead of traveling all the way to the feed store, which was a few miles out of town.

As she neared the door, it opened, and a young

woman came out. She paused when she saw Moira. "I'm sorry, ma'am, but we aren't open for business yet. I can run back inside and grab a pamphlet for you if you'd like, though."

"I'm actually the owner of the deli," Moira said. She gestured to her building. "Sorry, I just got excited when I saw that someone had started work on this place. I've been looking forward to meeting my new neighbors."

"Oh." The young woman brightened. "We actually have a gift basket for you. Come on in, you can meet my boss."

Moira followed her inside, unable to disguise her curiosity as she looked around the place. It was obvious that they were doing heavy renovating; the walls were half painted, there was drywall dust in the air, and uninstalled windows were leaning against one of the walls. Even so, she could already tell that the interior would be bright and spacious.

. . .

"This looks like it will be wonderful," she said. "What sort of stuff will you sell?"

"Well, we're primarily going to offer grooming and doggy daycare, but we'll also sell homemade dog treats as well as some food and toys. Do you have pets?"

"Two dogs," Moira replied. "I'm looking forward to having a doggy daycare right next door to the deli. I'm surprised I haven't heard anything about this place."

"We've been rushing to get everything ready," the young woman said. "My boss plans to open by Valentine's Day. I'm sorry, I didn't get your name."

"Oh, I'm Moira Darling."

"Darling's DELIcious Delights. Of course." The

young woman grinned. "I'm Penny. It's nice to meet you."

"It's nice to meet you too."

Penny opened a door and ushered her through. Moira found herself in a large, open room with a tiled floor and mats on the walls. Off to the right was a chain-link gate. Two men were installing the last few mats. One of them looked up, then said something to the other. They put the mat they were holding down and turned towards her and Penny.

"Wyatt, this is Ms. Darling. She owns the deli, and stopped by to introduce herself."

The older of the two men approached them. He had brown hair and wore an easy smile. His most striking feature, however, was that he was wearing an eye patch. Moira tried not to stare, but knew that she was failing miserably.

. . .

"Wyatt Merrick," he said, extending a hand. "And this is Andre, my nephew." The young man who had been helping him waved. "It's nice to meet you. I was going to stop by later today, but it looks like you beat me to it. I'm sure Penny told you what this place is?"

Moira shook his hand and tried to focus on his good eye. "Yes," she said. "A doggy daycare. It's a great idea."

"Don't worry about the sound. These mats are for soundproofing, so you shouldn't hear anything. We do have a small yard in back, but the dogs will be taken out individually and there's a privacy fence, so it shouldn't be an issue. We aren't zoned for overnight boarding or anything."

"I'm not worried about the noise," Moira assured him. She saw him relax a bit. "I just wanted to come say hi. I'm happy this building sold at last. If you want, I can put some of your business cards by the register at the deli."

. . .

17

He chuckled. "Well, we were going to ply you with a gift basket before asking that. Thank you, though. That's a very nice offer, and we'll definitely take you up on it."

"She has dogs," Penny said.

"Oh, you do? What breeds?"

"I've got a German shepherd and an Irish wolfhound," she said. "They're good dogs."

"Well, if they do well with other dogs, you're welcome to bring them here for daycare while you're at work."

"I'd love to," she said. She had often wished that she could bring the dogs to work with her occasionally, but knew that no matter how well behaved they were, it would never work out in a restaurant. "Sorry for interrupting, it looks like you guys are busy. I just wanted to say hi and see what sort of business this was. I should get going — the deli opens in about twenty minutes."

"Thanks for stopping in. I'm sure we'll be seeing more of each other. Penny, will you give her the gift basket on the way out?"

Moira followed the young woman back through the building, and waited in the entrance room while she grabbed a large gift basket out of an adjoining room. "Here you go," she said brightly. "We've got them for all of the surrounding businesses. I'm glad you stopped in. You guys serve lunch, right? I may stop by during my break."

"We start serving lunch at eleven. Our special today will be Italian orzo soup and club sandwiches, but we can make any sort of sandwich you'd like. I hope we'll see you. Are you related to Wyatt as well?"

Penny shook her head. "No. Wyatt and Andre are the

only two that are related. Me and one other girl work here now, and he's planning on hiring more people once we open. If you know anyone with grooming experience, send them our way."

"I don't think I do, but if I do think of anyone, I will," Moira said. She hefted the gift basket. "Thanks again."

She left, taking peeks at the gift basket as she returned to the deli. She had a feeling that she was going to like her new neighbors.

CHAPTER THREE

She got her wish for a slow day. After the first break-fast rush, when people stopped in for a coffee and a breakfast cookie on their way to work or school, business slowed down to a trickle. She managed to finish her book by ten, just in time to go back into the kitchen and start on the day's homemade soup.

Over the past few years, she had made nearly every kind of soup imaginable. From rich bisques, to hearty chowders, to cold summer soups, her favorites always seemed to include pasta. Today, she was making a vegetarian version of Italian wedding soup with orzo and vegetables. She took the biggest pot off its hook above the sink and put it on the stove before measuring out the vegetable broth. She set the burner to medium, and began to chop the vegetables while it heated up.

In the summer, she bought their produce fresh weekly from local farmers, but in the winter, it all had to be shipped in. Even though she knew there probably wasn't that much of a difference, she always thought that things didn't taste quite as good when they weren't local.

It wasn't long before the soup was bubbling away. She added the pasta, then remembering her desire to meet her husband's new business partner, she grabbed her phone and sent a text to David. *Everything is going so well*, she thought as she slipped the phone into her pocket. *David's finally going to be able to focus on the microbrewery like he's wanted to do for a long time, Candice and Ellie seem happy, even if they don't live nearby anymore, and I'm going to be able to begin bringing the dogs to doggy daycare while I'm working.* So far, the new year was going even better than she could have imagined.

· · ·

"Hey, Ms. D."

Moira jumped as Allison, one of her employees, walked into the kitchen. She had been so lost in thought that she hadn't heard her come in.

"Hey, Allison. How is everything?"

"Good. What's this?" she asked, looking at the gift basket that Moira had put on the employee table in the kitchen.

"That's from the people who are opening the new business next door. Did you notice the new sign when you came in?"

"I saw," the young woman said, sitting down at the table. "They put it up yesterday. Perfect Paws. What do they do?"

. . .

Moira told her. "They seem nice. Feel free to take anything out of there that you want. I don't need to eat so many chocolates, not unless I want to buy bigger pants."

"This is great," Allison said. "Are these cookies for dogs?"

"Yep. They have a small dog bakery too."

"I bet Keeva and Maverick will like them," Allison said. She dug around in the gift basket until she found a box of chocolates, which she opened. "Did Candice tell you about the trip we're planning this summer?"

"Not yet. Where are you planning on going?"

"Florida. We're going to go to a couple of amusement parks, and spend the rest of the time lounging on the beach. The plan is to bond as sisters, since, you know, we missed out on a lot of that."

Just a couple of months ago, Moira had discovered that her employee was actually her daughter's half-sister, from an affair that Candice's father had had a long time ago. It had been an emotional discovery for all of them, but she was glad for it. She had always regretted not giving Candice a sibling. While it was true that she and Allison had missed out on being able to grow up together, they already had a solid friendship. She was glad that the girls were embracing their newfound relationship.

"That sounds wonderful. I'm happy for both of you, and I'm sure you'll have a lot of fun." The bell on the door out front rang, and Moira waved a hand as Allison began to rise. "I'll get it. You can finish your chocolate, then give the soup a stir. It should be just about ready."

She left the kitchen and found Penny standing at the register. The young woman smiled at her brightly. "I managed to stop by. I'll have your special. I don't remember what you said it was, but it sounded good."

"It will be just a second," Moira said. "Do either of the others want anything?"

"Wyatt brought a lunch from home," Penny said. "And Andre left for the day, so they're good. Do you guys sell drinks too?"

"Yep, right over there."

While Penny examined the drink selection, Moira popped into the kitchen to give the order to Allison. She was just turning to head back to the counter and ring the order up when her cell phone buzzed in her pocket. She checked it and saw David's name on the screen. Reluctantly, she silenced the call. She had to take care of business first.

.   .   .

Once Penny left, she called David back, but he didn't answer. He had, however, left her a message that said simply, *Turn on the news.* Beginning to worry, she asked Allison to take over up front and grabbed her tablet out of her purse. She set it up on the table in the kitchen, pushing the gift basket out of the way, and searched for a website that had live local news. *I should get a TV for the kitchen*, she thought as she waited for the page to load.

What she saw pushed all idle thoughts out of her mind. With a banner that read, *Breaking News* floating across the bottom of the screen, the video showed a house with a multitude of police vehicles with flashing lights parked in front of it. She turned the volume up just in time to hear, "… confirmed shooting. The victim was found dead at the scene. The police received the first call at approximately ten-thirty this morning, with many other calls flooding in soon after. The quiet town of Lake Marion is flooded with chaos as the police begin the search for the shooter."

Moira took out her phone again and redialed David's

number. He answered on what must have been the last ring. "I'm sorry, Moira, I'm talking to the police. I can't talk for long."

"Who is it?" she asked, her voice shaking. If David was already involved with the police, the victim must have been someone they knew.

"His name was Rick Greene. He was a client of mine. We'll talk later, I just thought you should know what's going on. I might be home late."

"I understand," she said. "Be careful, okay, David? You're not in danger, right?"

"I don't think so," he said. "I just thought you should be aware. I've got to go now. They still have no idea who the shooter is, so I'm going to share everything from the case I was working on. I'll see you tonight."

They said their goodbyes, then David hung up.

Moira let her hand drop, and slid the phone into her pocket. Even though David had told her he was fine, she couldn't help but worry. Someone had shot and killed one of his clients. She didn't know what sort of case the man had hired David for, but she knew that even something as commonplace as a suspected affair could quickly escalate to violence. She just had to hope that her husband wouldn't be the next target.

CHAPTER FOUR

She spent the rest of the day at the deli checking her phone as frequently as possible, hoping for an update from her husband. When she had time for a break, she turned her tablet back on and returned to the news website, hoping to learn that the shooter had been caught. The story hadn't been updated for hours, and she tried to hide her disappointment as she closed the page. By then, news of the shooting had spread, and it was all anyone was talking about. Lake Marion and Maple Creek were both small towns, and something as violent as an unsolved shooting would be the talk of the towns for weeks. Moira hadn't told anyone that David had a connection to the case.

.   .   .

The murder made her happier than ever that David was taking a step back from his private investigating business. If he kept at it, she worried that one day he would be targeted for whatever role he had played in bringing down someone's marriage, or revealing an important secret. Running a microbrewery had to be a much safer profession than following people who didn't want to be followed.

It was late by the time she made it home. While she enjoyed being at the deli, twelve-hour shifts were tiring. With Darrin gone, she would have to pull more full days than she wanted to, but she knew that giving him the vacation time had been the right thing to do. His parents had gone on a cruise to celebrate thirty years of marriage, and he had been the only one they trusted to watch their animals and house while they were gone. She knew that if she were in his shoes, she would have appreciated the time off as well. Her employees were the backbone of her business, and she did what she could to keep them happy and let them know that she appreciated them.

. . .

The house was dark, and David's car wasn't in the driveway. He had told her that he would probably be late, so she tried not to worry too much as she turned on all the lights and let the dogs out. She had brought home leftover soup for dinner, but knew that she wouldn't have any appetite for it until David was back. *I hate this*, she thought. There was nothing worse than worrying about her family's safety.

The thought gave her chills. If someone wanted to target her husband, then the logical place for them to start would be at his house. She shoved the bag holding the cups of soup into the fridge and returned to the front door, making sure that the deadbolt was turned, and the porch light was on. Then she walked back through the kitchen to let the dogs in, not bothering to lock them in the mudroom while their feet dried. She felt better with the dogs with her. Both of them were large and had intimidating barks, and she knew that Maverick, at least, would protect her if he needed to.

She didn't know what to do with herself while she

waited. She grabbed a library book from the counter, but couldn't get past the first paragraph. In the end, cleaning was what kept her sane. She finished everything that had been on her list that she hadn't gotten done yesterday, and was about to start cleaning the oven when her phone rang. She jumped up and grabbed it off the counter, relieved to see David's number.

"Hello?"

"Hey," he said. "I'm on my way home. I'm bringing Lenny, and I just thought I should let you know. He and I need to go over the case again. I'm sure there's something that can point us toward the culprit."

"Lenny?"

"My new partner," he said. "I forgot you hadn't met him yet. We're picking up Chinese food now. Do you want anything?"

· · ·

"Just a couple of egg rolls," she said. "I've got soup here. I'll see you guys soon?"

"I'll drive straight there, and Lenny will be right behind me. It will be about fifteen minutes."

She breathed a sigh of relief. They said their good-byes and she hung up. David was all right, and by the sound of it, he was with his new business partner, so he wasn't alone. *At least the house is clean now*, she thought, looking around. They didn't have people over very often, not now that Candice lived a couple of hours away, so she tried to mentally look at her home from a stranger's point of view. David might not care much about that sort of thing, but she wanted to make a good first impression on this Lenny. By the sound of it, he would be a part of their lives for a long time to come.

How can David do it? she wondered as she went upstairs to freshen up. *I can't imagine having a business partner for the deli. What if we disagreed about something important?* She knew that David still cared about the business, even if he was taking a step back from it. He had built it from the ground up. How could he not? She told herself that he must really like Lenny, if he was willing to trust him to take over the daily operations.

By the time the two cars pulled into the driveway, Moira was ready. She had brushed out her hair, changed her clothes, and had even put on a spritz of perfume. When the dogs began to bark, she called them into the kitchen and gated them in the mudroom, so Lenny wouldn't have to contend with the two of them vying for his attention.

"I'm glad you're home," she said as she opened the front door a minute later. David was standing on the porch, with a thin, balding man next to him. "I was worried, after what I saw on the news."

"I know, and I'm sorry. I still can't believe what happened. Rick seemed like a good guy. I just hope it didn't have anything to do with the case." Her husband gestured to the man beside him. "This is Lenny Picard. Lenny, this is my wife, Moira."

"It's nice to meet you," Lenny said, shaking her hand. "I've heard so much about you."

"It's nice to meet you too. Come on in, it's cold out there."

Lenny pushed his glasses further up his nose, then walked past her into the house. David paused to give her a quick kiss, then followed him, a bag of Chinese food in his hand. Moira shut and locked the door behind them.

"Here, I'll take the food into the kitchen while you give Lenny a tour," she said. "I'll get plates out for everyone too. What do you want to drink?"

. . .

"I'll have a beer," David said. "Lenny?"

"Beer sounds good to me. It's been that sort of day. Thanks."

Moira took the food into the kitchen and began getting plates and silverware out of the cupboards and drawers. Lenny wasn't what she had expected, but he seemed nice so far. She just hoped that he was everything that David seemed to hope for — but then, David had always been a good judge of character.

At last, the three of them sat down to eat, Moira with her eclectic soup and egg rolls, and the other two with their noodles and orange chicken. She still wasn't very hungry, but the two men obviously were. She waited until they took a few bites before asking something that she had wondered ever since David had told her that the murdered man had been a client.

. . .

"So, the guy that died... Rick... what sort of case were you working on for him?"

"He thought that he was being followed," David said. "So he hired me, well, us, to tail him and see what we could find out. I hate to admit it, but I thought that he was imagining things. That's why I figured it would be an easy case for Lenny to start out with. No offense."

"None taken," Lenny assured him. "I don't mind starting off easy. It's been a while since I've solved anything besides where a missing sock went."

"Do you have any experience with this sort of stuff?" Moira asked, unable to help but wonder what her husband saw in the man.

"I do. I got my PI's license years ago, and actually opened up my own office. Then, I got married. I ended up setting all the private investigating stuff aside, so I could work a more stable job and make enough money to take care of my family. Now, my daughter's out of college and can support herself, and my ex-wife is living in Wisconsin with her new husband, so I figured I might as well follow my own dreams for once. I saw David's ad in the newspaper, and decided to answer it. Of course, this wasn't quite how I envisioned my first case going."

"So, what happened, exactly?" Moira asked. "Does this mean that your client was right, and someone really was following him?"

"It might," David said with a sigh. "Lenny was supposed to start following him this morning."

"He had already been killed by the time I got there," Lenny said. "The first police car showed up just as I did. I feel terrible. If I had gotten there just a few minutes earlier, I might have seen the person who did it." He popped another piece of chicken into his mouth.

. . .

"I'm sorry," Moira said. "This must be terrible for both of you. Is there anything I can do?"

"I don't think so. It was a new case, so we don't have much to go over besides what he told me when I met with him. Feel free to join us if you want. Three heads are better than two."

CHAPTER FIVE

Even with the three of them talking about the case for over an hour, no headway was made. Rick Greene had told David that a man in a dark colored car had been following him around town for the past week. Unfortunately, that wasn't much to go on. David had done a background check on his client to see if he had any criminal records that might indicate that he was in some sort of trouble, but had come up with nothing. It was all the same stuff that the police would do as well, but she knew her husband felt better doing it himself. Lenny seemed to feel the same way; once they started going through the man's records, he was all business.

. . .

It was late when Lenny finally said goodbye, and Moira and David went straight to bed afterward. She didn't have a twelve hour shift the next day, but she *did* have to wake up early again for a morning shift. *Darrin needs a raise*, she thought as she settled against her pillow. *I don't know how he manages to wake up so early to go into work without complaining. I own the place, and I'm already getting tired of it on day two.*

She had promised to meet up with her two best friends later that day, so even though she was tired from staying up so late the night before, she headed over to Denise's house after work. There, she and her friends relaxed in the living room with a platter of cookies and a couple of plates of finger sandwiches, plus a bottle of the Redwood Grill's house wine. It had been a while since she had had the opportunity to completely relax with her friends, so she pushed all thoughts of the murder out of her mind as they chatted, the TV playing quietly in the background.

"Your house is so nice," Martha groaned. She

reached for a cookie, changed her mind, and grabbed a cucumber sandwich instead. "I'm jealous, I'll admit it."

Denise laughed. "Don't be. I only have this place because I won it in the divorce. It's not exactly something to be proud of. And I've been to your house, Martha. It's just as nice."

"I'm just jealous of your kitchen," Moira said. "I'd love to have a restaurant quality kitchen in my house. Not that I cook much at home. We eat way too much takeout. I need to make a resolution to cook more."

"Trust me, mine doesn't get used as much as you'd think," Denise said. "Logan usually orders delivery for dinner, and by the time I get home from a day at the Grill, it's all I can do to grab a slice of pizza before heading to bed. Of course, I made the cookies this morning, which was nice. I so rarely get a day off. I'm glad I can trust Julian to keep things under control while I'm not there."

.   .   .

"Where is Logan?" Moira asked. "I don't see much of him anymore."

"He's at work right now," Denise said. "He got a job at the auto shop — you know, that place that Edna used to run before she passed away."

"That's good, I'm glad he found somewhere to work. I feel bad that I didn't offer him a place at the deli, but after what happened..." She trailed off. Logan was Denise's nephew, and had been arrested the year before after killing someone in what he thought had been self-defense. The case had been complicated, and Logan had spent months in prison before getting out after an appeal.

"I understand," Denise said. "Don't worry, Moira. I know it's hard to look at him the same way you did before. I mean, he's my nephew, and I still have a hard time thinking about... what happened." Her friend took a deep breath. "I haven't talked about it with anyone, you know? Not even with him. Both of us just kind of pretended that it didn't happen when he first got back, and now, after so long, it would be weird to bring it up. I just want him to be happy and be able to move on, but whenever I look at him, I can't help but think of that man he killed."

"That man was stalking me," Moira said. "And he was dangerous. I know, though, it's hard. I'm sorry for bringing it up. We should talk about something happier. It sounds like things are going well with you and Julian."

"They are." Denise smiled. "I forgot what it was like to spend time with a man who actually enjoys being around me. I guess I just kind of forgot what normal was, after all of my bad experiences with my ex-husband. I'm glad I met Julian. How are things with Damien, Martha?"

"I think we're done seeing each other," their other friend said casually. She reached for the table again, and grabbed a cookie this time. Moira and Denise exchanged a look.

"Why?" Denise said.

"Honestly? The magic is just gone. Maybe I'm not meant to get married." She shrugged.

"Are you okay?" Moira asked. "There were, well, more tears at your last breakup."

"The thing is, it wasn't even a breakup. Not with tears and screaming and all of that. We just got to seeing each other a lot less, and eventually I told him I wanted to put things on hold for a while, and he said okay, and that was it. Maybe I'm finally getting old enough that drama won't be a part of dating anymore. You know, I actually ran into someone at the grocery store the other day that I liked a lot." She grinned. "No ring, so I don't think he's married. He's cute, even though he wears an eye patch."

. . .

The deli owner sat up straighter. "An eye patch? Are you talking about Wyatt?"

"How do *you* know him?" Martha asked.

"He bought the building next to the deli. He's the one opening the doggy daycare."

"Tell me everything," Martha said, shifting on the couch so she was facing her friend. "And I mean everything."

Laughing, Moira began to relate her visit to Perfect Paws to her friend. They talked about Wyatt until Denise cleared her throat and turned up the volume on the television.

"Guys," she said. "Check this out."

. . .

"I'm coming to you live from a scene of shocking violence," the news reporter said, standing in front of a row of police cars. Behind her, Moira could see a vehicle that had run headfirst into a tree. "This is the second mystery shooting in two days. The perpetrator has not been caught, and once again, the victim has been declared dead at the scene. This time, however, we have a witness — a local private investigator who was following the victim when the incident occurred."

Moira tensed, expecting to see David on the television, but instead the person that the camera panned over to was Lenny. The reporter asked him, "Could you tell us what you saw?"

"Um, a dark car — maybe black or dark blue — came around the corner." He licked his lips nervously, and seemed unable to decide whether to look at the camera or the reporter while he was speaking. Instead, he looked back and forth between the two. "It was coming from the other direction, and drove right past the... the victim. I saw someone stick a gun out the window and I heard two loud bangs.

Then the victim's car swerved into the guard rail, and I stopped and called the police." There was a long pause. "That's it," he added.

The camera refocused on the reporter. "So, there we have it. Keep your eyes peeled for someone with a gun in a dark blue or black car. If you see anything suspicious, please call the number at the bottom of the screen. Do not — and I repeat — do *not* approach this person. They are armed and should be considered very dangerous."

CHAPTER SIX

"I want you to stop working on this case," Moira said.

It was evening, and David had just gotten home after another long day of speaking to the police. He was alone this time, which was good because the conversation that she wanted to have with him was one that they couldn't have in front of Lenny.

"What case?" he asked, raising an eyebrow as he reached for a coat hanger.

.   .   .

"The one that involves the people who keep getting shot."

"They're different cases, Moira." He hung his coat up and shut the closet door, shaking his head as he turned back toward her. "Two completely different cases."

"What do you mean?" she asked, blinking. She had been certain that this most recent murder must have had something to do with Rick Greene's death.

"This last person that died, Michael Bronn, he was part of a completely different case than the one we had taken on for Rick. Michael's wife hired us to tail him because she thought he was having an affair. As far as I know, the two men didn't know each other at all."

"But... the dark colored car. There has to be a connection."

. . .

"Let's sit down and talk about this," he said. "It's been a long day. I need some coffee."

She followed him into the kitchen where she sat at the table while he poured himself a cup of coffee. He joined her after a moment. "I agree that there must be some sort of connection, but I can assure you that the connection has nothing to do with me. I know you're worried, but I'm trying to train Lenny. I can't just stop taking cases until the shooter is caught."

"But David, what if they target you next? This person has a gun. He isn't playing around. If he drives up behind you and — well, look at what happened today."

"I know." He covered her hand with his. "Moira, I'll be careful. But I honestly think the fact that both of these people had ties to one of my cases is a coincidence. I don't want you to worry. I wasn't even there either time. Lenny was the one that found them."

.   .   .

Moira inhaled sharply. Lenny. David was right; both murders had occurred when Lenny had been following the victims.

"What color car does he drive?" she asked.

"Lenny? It's black."

She stared at him. "David, the first victim said he was being followed by a someone driving a dark car."

David shook his head. "Moira, Lenny witnessed the second murder, remember? I know what you're thinking, but it isn't him. I drive a black car too. A lot of people do."

"Does he have a gun?"

Her husband shifted, not meeting her gaze.

. . .

"Does he?"

He sighed. "He does. And yes, he has a license to carry it concealed. I suggested that he keep it on him while working cases, just in case."

Moira stood up, her chair scraping across the tiles. She began to pace back and forth in the kitchen. "So, he has a black car and carries a gun, and he was at the scene of both murders, and you don't think that's even a little bit suspicious?"

David sighed. "I can see why it would look that way. Look, he didn't even get to Rick's house until after the police had been called. The police themselves confirmed that. And he was tailing Michael when he was shot. If he wanted to lie about that, he would have said that the shooter's car came from behind them. The police will be able to trace the trajectory of the bullets, and he knows that. If he shot Michael while he was following him, the bullets would have a different trajectory than they would if he had been shot from the side or front."

"So, he was lying about following the guy," she said. "Are there any witnesses that saw him tailing Michael?"

David frowned. "No. Not that I know of."

She fell silent, but stared at him. She knew that he had to be making the same connections that she was. Her husband was the one that made a living out of solving mysteries, after all.

"I just... I don't think he's the type," he said after a minute. "His background check was clean. His references check out. He's not in debt, he doesn't have any sort of history that might indicate a violent past. Why would he want to kill these people? He didn't even choose these cases. I gave them to him. I can imagine what it looks like, if you're looking at it from the outside. But without a motive, there's no case. If he wasn't involved at all and I was the one who had been at the scene both times, would you think it was me?"

"No. Of course not. But I know you so much better than you know him. Just..." She sighed. "Be careful okay? Be careful around him. I love you, and if something happened to you, I don't know how I could live with it."

"Hey," he said. He stood up and pulled her into his arms. "It's okay. I love you too, and I'll be careful. I promise. What are you doing tomorrow morning?"

"Working." She made a face, even though she knew he couldn't see it. Rising before the sun was not her strong suit. "But I'm free in the afternoon. Why?"

"Let's take the dogs and go on a nice walk somewhere. It's supposed to be a bit warmer, and I think we could both use the chance to get outside. I already told Lenny to take the day off, and Karissa will be at the brewery, so it will just be the two of us and the dogs, with no worries."

"Okay," she said. "That sounds like a good plan. I'll stop home after work and we can drive out to the trails together."

CHAPTER SEVEN

David had been right; it was a warm day, with temperatures in the forties — the perfect sort of day to hit the trails after being cooped up from months of bitterly cold temperatures. Maple Creek was in northern Michigan, and was surrounded by forests on all sides. That day, she and David simply drove until they found a small roadside park with trail access. They pulled in and parked alongside two other vehicles; a white minivan, and a dark green sedan with a white paw print decal on the rear window that she thought looked familiar. Moira opened thc rear hatch and grabbed the dogs' leashes as they jumped out, both of them wriggling with excitement.

. . .

"Do you want Maverick or Keeva?" she asked.

"You choose," he said.

She handed him Maverick's leash and set off down the trail, pausing only to hit the button on her keychain to lock her SUV. Just because Maple Creek was a small town didn't mean that there wasn't a criminal element around — a fact which had been highlighted by the recent shootings. Taking a deep breath, she pushed down the twinge of unease she felt as she thought about the two deaths. She had made a promise to herself that she wouldn't focus on that, not today. The more she thought about it, the more she worried about her husband, and worrying wouldn't do either of them any good.

"Which way?" she asked when they reached the first fork.

"It looks like Maverick's choosing for us," David said, laughing as the German shepherd pulled him down the trail. Moira grinned and followed with Keeva. It felt wonderful to be doing something active, and she was glad that David had had the idea.

Once they had gotten about ten minutes into their hike, David reached down and unclipped Maverick's leash. The German shepherd was used to romping through the five acres of woods that she and David owned, and was pretty good about sticking around.

"Just keep an eye out for other hikers," she warned her husband. "Remember, there were two other vehicles parked in the lot. I don't want him to bother anyone."

"He'll be fine," David said, reaching down to ruffle the dog's ears. "Go on, boy. Have fun."

Maverick took off, dashing a few yards ahead before stopping to snuffle at a half-melted pile of snow. Keeva tugged at her leash and whined. Moira reached down to pat the dog. The Irish wolfhound wasn't as reliable off leash, and even though she felt bad for her, she didn't want to chance the dog running away.

"Sorry, sweetie," she said. "Maybe one day."

"So," David said as they started walking again. "Our trip. Where do you want to go?"

Moira paused. She hadn't thought about their planned Valentine's Day trip at all. With everything else that had happened, it had slipped her mind. She didn't want to let David know, though; he had seemed excited for it. She was too, but worry for her husband had made everything else seem unimportant.

"Let's go to Chicago," she said, going with the first thing that came to mind. She relaxed into her idea as she realized it was a good one. "We can go to the aquarium, see some museums, go to some nice restaurants, and stay in whatever hotel has the best room service."

He grinned. "If we can have five-star meals delivered to our door, I think we might never leave the room. I think it sounds like a good idea, though. I haven't been to Chicago in years."

"Me either," she said. "It's close enough that we can drive down in a day, so we won't have to set aside too much time for travel or try to schedule a flight and rent a car on such short notice. Plus, we can visit Candice on our way back home."

"Let's look at hotel reservations when we get home," he said. "I'm looking forward to it."

"Me too." She reached over with her free hand and took his. She really was looking forward to their weekend away together. In just a week and a half, she would be lounging in a luxurious suite with her husband by her side and not a single care in the world.

Except the murders. Her face fell. What if the culprit wasn't caught by then? What if David left his private investigating business in Lenny's hands while they were gone, and he committed another crime? Somehow, she didn't think that the killer would stop at two murders. Someone who killed so easily and so quickly must have had practice. The only question was, who would be next on his list?

Maverick barked, jolting her out of her thoughts. She called the dog back automatically. When he ignored her, she tried again, this time with a sharper tone.

"Maverick, come here."

The German shepherd gave a low grumble and trotted back to her. She grabbed his collar while David clipped the leash on. She could hear the jingling now; someone else was approaching along the trail, and it sounded like they had a dog with them.

They didn't have long to wait before the person rounded the corner. Moira's eyes went to the dog first, and she smiled when she saw a neatly groomed standard poodle trotting along beside its owner. Then her eyes found the man's face, and she jolted with surprise. It was a face she recognized easily even from this distance, thanks to the eye patch. Wyatt.

"You okay?" David murmured, looking at her with concern.

"Yeah," she said. "I just didn't expect to see someone I know out here."

"You know him?"

. . .

Moira realized that with all of the craziness surrounding the murders, she had completely forgotten to tell David about the new business next to the deli. She caught him up in a hurried whisper as Wyatt drew closer to them.

"Oh, hi," he said, pausing a few feet away from them. "Ms. Darling, isn't it?"

"You can call me Moira," she said. "Wyatt, this is my husband, David."

"It's nice to meet you." The two men shook hands. Between them, the dogs were engaged in their own greeting.

"It looks like they like each other," Wyatt said, glancing down at his poodle, who was sniffing Keeva's ear. "Your dogs are beautiful. I hope you bring them to daycare. They seem like they'd be a good fit. They're certainly friendly."

. . .

"They are," Moira said with a smile. "The German shepherd is Maverick, and the wolfhound is Keeva. They're good dogs."

"This is Stanford. He's not as dignified as his name sounds, though." He stroked the poodle's head. "Well, our daycare room is set up. You can bring them over tomorrow morning if you'd like and we can introduce them to Penny's dogs to see how they do in a group. If it goes well, we can sign you up. You'll be our first customer. I'll give you guys a great discount, of course. It will be good to have some good reviews already up by the time we officially open."

"Great," she said. "I'll bring them by. Thanks again. I'm sure they'll be happier playing with other dogs all day instead of staying home alone all day."

Her phone rang, and she checked it automatically. It was Candice. Wyatt seemed to take the call as his cue to leave.

. . .

"I'll see you tomorrow. It was nice to meet you, David."

He waved, and continued on his way down the path, going the direction they had just come from. Moira answered the call, excited to speak with her daughter. Candice was living her own life now, and Moira knew she had to be okay with that, but she still missed the closeness that they had shared in the past.

"Hey, Mom," her daughter said, sounding cheerful.

David took her arm gently, and they began to walk again as she talked. "Hi, sweetie. How are you?"

"I'm great. My boss is out of town for a month, and he left me completely in charge of the store, plus I'm getting a raise. I know it's not the same as running my own shop, but honestly, it's less stressful and I have way more time to focus on other stuff. Eli got a job too."

. . .

"Oh, where? How is his physical therapy coming along?"

"He's working at a bookstore. He likes it, but I can tell he misses the ice cream shop. And he's doing well, he actually had his last session last week. He's still got a limp, but it's way better than it could have been. I'm just happy that he can walk."

"That's great," Moira said. "Allison told me about the trip you girls are planning. It sounds like it will be fun."

"It will. I'm excited for it. Anyway, I called because I want to come visit this weekend. Eli can't, because he has to work, and he doesn't want to ask for time off so soon after getting the new job, so it will just be me, but I still want to visit Reggie and everything. Can I stay with you guys?"

. . .

"Of course," Moira answered automatically. "You know there's always a bed for you in our house."

"Great. I just thought I should check since..."

Moira listened only vaguely as her daughter chattered in her ear. She had just had a sickening realization. There was still a murderer on the loose somewhere in town. He had killed two people so far, and both had been connected to her husband's work. What if he decided to target David next? Even worse, what if her daughter got caught in the crossfire? She hadn't been worried about it when Candice was out of town, but the visit might put her in danger.

"Mom?"

"Huh?"

"Were you even listening?"

. . .

"Yeah, of course. I'm just in the middle of a hike with David and the dogs. Sorry. Sweetie —"

"Oh, can I talk to David? I didn't know he was there. I want to say hi."

Moira handed the phone over to her husband, using the time that he spent talking to his stepdaughter to think. Was it safe for Candice to visit that weekend? *What if the shooter is never caught? I can't have her stay away forever. And David is usually right about this sort of thing. If he doesn't think there's a connection, then he's probably right.*

David handed the phone back to her after a moment. She took a deep breath. She wouldn't forbid Candice from visiting — not that she could, her daughter was an adult, after all — but she *would* tell the young woman what was going on. She could make her own, educated choice.

. . .

"Before you go," she said, "there's something I have to tell you..."

She told her daughter all about the murders, and was unsurprised when Candice said that she wanted to visit anyway. She was left with a worried feeling in the pit of her stomach as she said goodbye and hung up. If Candice got hurt, she knew that she would never be able to forgive herself.

CHAPTER EIGHT

Moira pulled up in front of Perfect Paws the next morning, her mind still on her daughter's visit. Two murders in two days was frightening, and it wasn't the sort of situation she wanted the person that she loved most in the world to be walking into, but Candice had been adamant that she still wanted to visit. She knew that she would be worried until her daughter was safely on her way home, but she didn't want to wreck the visit completely. *I just need to think about something else,* she told herself. *Like making sure that Keeva and Maverick are on their best behavior.*

She got out of the SUV and walked around to the rear hatch. She held up a finger, giving the dogs a stern look through the window. They both loved going new places, and were beside themselves with excitement. She wished she could impress on them just how important this meeting went. If they could start coming to doggy daycare, it would add a whole new facet to their lives. The dogs often got the short end of the stick, when it came to her and David's busy lives, and she wanted to change that.

"Be good," she said as she carefully opened the hatch, grabbing at their leashes so they couldn't dart out. "I mean it. Don't jump on anyone, don't push the other dogs around, and Maverick — don't you dare lift your leg on anything."

She let them out of the car and led them into the building, passing by a green car with a white paw print decal. *That's where I remembered it from,* she thought. *This must be Wyatt's car.* The interior of the building had been transformed in the few short days since she had last visited. The walls in the front room were now completely painted, and the fixtures had been installed. There was a large glass window to the side of the front desk, which looked in on the daycare room. Through the window, Moira could see a couple of dogs playing, supervised by Penny. She wasn't sure what to do next. Should she just go in? There wasn't a bell on the desk, and no one else was in the front room.

A door off to the side opened, and Andre, Wyatt's nephew walked through. He looked surprised for a moment, then seemed to remember who she was.

"You're here to introduce the dogs, right? I'll show you in. Right through here."

He opened the door to the daycare area, and Moira found herself behind a chain-link gate. The door behind her clicked shut, and the dogs that were playing in the room, including Wyatt's poodle, Stanford, rushed up to the gate.

"I guess this is like a practice tour for us," Andre said, giving her a nervous smile. "So, there's always at least two gates between the dogs and the outside.

That's to make sure none of them get loose and run into the street. We always make sure the first gate — or door in this case — is closed before opening the second one. Introductions are done off leash." He waited while she unclipped Keeva and Maverick. "Usually with new dogs, we introduce them one at a time to make sure they don't have any major behavioral issues first, but my uncle said he already met your dogs, so that's fine. We'll just open this gate and let them into the room."

He reached around her and did just that. Keeva and Maverick paused for a moment, looking back at her as if they weren't quite sure they had permission, then trotted forward to sniff the other dogs.

"They seem fine," Andre said. "The poodle is Stanford, my uncle's dog, and the two mixed breed dogs are Nikki and Taco — they're Penny's."

"It's nice that she gets to bring them to work," Moira said. She walked into the room, and Andre followed her, closing the gate behind her. "Do you have dogs?"

"No. I've never actually owned a dog. I only got this job because my uncle offered it to me. Don't worry, though, I like dogs, and I'm learning a lot."

She watched as the dogs, their sniffing done, began to race around the room. Penny watched them for a moment, a smile on her face, then walked over to greet Moira.

"Hey. I'm glad you could make it this morning. I know we aren't completely set up yet, but I think Wyatt's glad that we have at least one customer. Do you want to see the rest of the place? The grooming room's a bit of a mess still, but I want some practice giving tours before we start getting real customers." She paused. "Not that you're not a real customer, but I guess it's different with you since you own the business right beside ours. Sorry, I'm making a mess of things, aren't I?"

.   .   .

"Not at all," Moira said, laughing. "Go ahead with the tour."

"I was going to show her around," Andre said.

"I want to do it," Penny said. "You're Wyatt's nephew, he's not going to fire you if you mess up once or twice. But he might fire me. I really want the practice. Please?"

Andre opened his hands, giving up, and turned to watch the dogs. Moira followed Penny to the right, toward another chain link gate. The young woman opened it and led her into a room that was filled with boxes.

"So, this is where all of the grooming will be done. That door there leads to a hallway that goes back to the front room, so we don't have to lead grooming dogs through the daycare area. We're getting some kennels set up over the weekend, and each one will have a dog bed in it, as well as no-spill water dishes that attach to the doors, so we can take more than one dog at once."

Moira followed the young woman around, smiling as Penny talked rapidly, describing everything within sight to her. They walked back through the daycare room to the door to outside, where she found herself in a small yard. The ground was covered with gravel, and the double fence — with a layer of chain link on the inside and a wooden privacy fence on the outside — stood a good foot above her head.

"Well, that's about it," Penny said at last. "I mean, there's the storage room and the break room, and Wyatt's office, but I don't think any of those are on the official tour. I could still show them to you if you wanted. Do you have any questions?"

"I don't," Moira said. "This all looks wonderful. I'm sure my dogs will enjoy coming here, and I'm looking forward to having them right next door while I'm working. You've completely sold me as a customer."

"Thanks." Penny beamed at her. "You have no idea how much I wanted this job. I love dogs, and I've always wanted to work with animals, so when I saw the job listing, I was *so* excited. I even get to bring my dogs to work with me, can you believe it?"

"It seems like it will be an amazing job," Moira said. "And Wyatt seems nice. I'm sure he'll be a great boss."

"He is. Once you get past the eye patch, he's a totally cool guy."

"Do you know why he wears it?" Moira asked. She knew it was likely a very personal matter, but couldn't help her curiosity.

"I think it's something that happened to him when

he was younger. I know he's missing the eye. I kept staring at it, and he offered to take it off, but I was too squeamish. Andre knows, but I don't want to ask him. I don't think he'd tell me, anyway. He's super devoted to his uncle. All I know is that he got into trouble years ago, and Wyatt got him out of it somehow."

They fell silent, until Moira realized that she had to hurry. "I'd better get going if I want to drop the dogs off at home before coming back into town for work," she said.

"Oh, you can leave them here for a few hours if you want," Penny said. "Wyatt will be here soon, so between him and Andre and I, someone will always be watching the dogs. We've pretty much just got to unpack the grooming room today; it won't be hard work or anything."

"Are you sure?"

. . .

"Yeah. It doesn't make sense for you to drive all the way back to your house and then return to the deli. It'll be like practice for when they start coming here for the whole day."

"Well, thank you," Moira said, shaking the young woman's hand. "This is wonderful, and I'm excited to watch this place grow."

CHAPTER NINE

Moira cracked open the slow cooker's lid, eying the brisket inside. The slow cooker had made her resolution to begin cooking outside of the deli more much easier. It was as simple as putting all of the ingredients together in the morning, then checking the food when she got home in the evening. It was perfect for a busy Saturday like this, when she was getting home from work only an hour before her daughter was supposed to arrive.

"Are you sure I shouldn't cancel with Lenny?" David called from the other room.

. . .

"It will be nice to spend some time one on one with Candice," she called back. She shut the slow cooker and left the kitchen to find David in the living room, focused on his laptop. "But of course, if you wanted to reschedule, we'd love to have you here."

"I really shouldn't," he sighed. "I thought she was getting here earlier, or I wouldn't have told Lenny to handle it on his own, but this person he's been following has been stealing from a lot of people he's worked for. Three of them actually came together to hire us to catch him in the act, and Lenny's convinced that he's meeting his fence at this bar to get rid of the stolen goods, so we have to be there."

"It's fine," she told David. "Trust me, Candice will understand. You can always catch up with her tomorrow."

"I know. I just feel bad, she hasn't visited in a while. But if I'm going to do this, I'd better head out. I'll text you when I'm on my way home, okay?"

. . .

"Okay," she said. "Be careful."

She still didn't trust Lenny completely. It had been less than a week since the first shooting, and the police hadn't made any headway into the case — at least, not that had been on the news. David had spent a lot of time with his new business partner over the past few days, and she told herself that if there was anything off about the man, David would have noticed. Still, she couldn't shake the coincidences. Lenny had been nearby both times someone had been shot, and he drove the right kind of car.

"I always am," her husband said. "Have a nice time with Candice."

He got up, put his laptop in his briefcase, and kissed her goodbye. Moira watched him leave with a bad feeling in her stomach, but pushed it aside for the time being. There was nothing she could do about David going to meet with Lenny, and she knew that she was probably worrying about nothing. Instead, she wanted to focus on getting ready for Candice's visit.

She had already washed the bedding in the spare room, even though she didn't think anyone had stayed there since the last time her daughter had spent the night. There was a stock of Candice's favorite drinks in the fridge, and some of the snacks she remembered her daughter liking in the pantry. As she began mixing the brownie batter in the kitchen, Moira admitted to herself that she might have gone a little bit overboard. Candice was only staying until Sunday evening, after all.

By the time the dogs started barking, signaling Candice's arrival, Moira had the table set, the brownies were minutes away from coming out of the oven, and the brisket, creamed corn, and salad were all on the table. She took one last look at everything, then pulled a bottle of chilled wine out of the fridge and set it on the table. Now it was perfect. She allowed herself a quick grin, then hurried to open the door.

. . .

She embraced her daughter for a long moment before finally pulling back. Candice's hair was shorter, and she had added a swoop of long bangs. Besides that, she looked the same as the last time Moira had seen her. *It hasn't been that long,* she told herself. *It's only been since Christmas.*

"You look great," she said aloud. "I love the hair."

"Thanks. There's a hair salon right next to where I work, and they're always bringing over coupons, so I decided to give it a try."

"Come the rest of the way in," Moira said. "Go ahead and put your stuff in your room, then I've got dinner waiting on the table."

Candice joined her in the kitchen a few minutes later. Moira was taking the brownies out of the oven, glad that they had turned out perfectly.

· · ·

89

"So, where's David?" her daughter asked, sitting down in one of the chairs. "The table's only set for two."

"He had to go do a work thing," Moira said. "But don't worry, he'll be back later tonight, and he's got the entire day free tomorrow. The three of us will go and see Reggie together — I thought we could have lunch with him if you wanted."

"Sure. I want to stop by the house too, and see how things are going. I know Thelma said she wanted to start looking into buying a place this spring, so I'm going to talk with her about a month-to-month lease agreement."

"Sounds good," Moira said. "Let's eat now, before everything gets cold."

It was nice, eating dinner with her daughter, just the two of them like it had been for so many years. She was happy in her new life with David, but she'd be lying to herself if she said that she didn't miss the years she had spent raising Candice. Everything had changed so quickly. She had gone from being focused on being a mother, working a part-time job, and living in the same house she had lived in since before Candice was born, to running a quickly expanding business, moving, and getting married, all within the space of a couple of years. Now that Candice lived in a different town altogether, the change was even more obvious. Her daughter had taken up such a huge part of her life, and she still hadn't completely filled that hole. She doubted that she ever would — Candice was the most important thing in the world to her, after all.

"That was great, Mom," her daughter said when they were done with dinner. "I was expecting soup or something, not like a huge meal."

"I've been trying to branch out with my cooking lately. I realize that I'd gotten into this rut where all I do is cook soup and slice up deli meats for sandwiches, and I'd forgotten that I actually like cooking other things too. We've still got brownies. Do you have room? I bought ice cream too."

"How could I turn down brownies and ice cream? Here, I'll start clearing the table while you get the ice cream out."

Moira had just begun to cut the brownies when her phone rang. It was late enough that she knew any incoming call must be important, so she excused herself and grabbed her phone. She was surprised to see David's number. She hadn't expected him to be done with work until much later.

"Hey," she said, already smiling. If he was on his way home, she would ask Candice to wait to eat the brownies until he got there.

"Moira, I know you're going to worry, so I'll just start by saying I'm completely fine."

. . .

"David? What happened?"

"There was another shooting tonight, at the bar I was supposed to meet Lenny at."

She inhaled sharply. "Oh, my goodness. Were you there when it happened? Did anyone get hurt?"

"It happened right before I arrived. And yes, the victim passed away."

"Oh, no," she said. "That's terrible. I'm so sorry. Was it the person you were tailing?"

"No," David said.

Moira felt a rush of relief. At least this time the murder wasn't connected to her husband in any way. "Still, that's horrible. Who was it?"

.   .   .

"I didn't catch his name, but it's no one we know. Moira, there's one more thing..." He hesitated. When he spoke again, his voice was lower. "Lenny was there. He had arrived before me, and was in the bar when the incident happened. I don't know what happened exactly, but even though my gut is still telling me otherwise, you're right. The coincidence is just too much. He must have something to do with all of this."

"I'm sorry," Moira said. "I know you like him, and that you thought you'd found someone you could rely on."

"Trust me, I'm even more disappointed than you are." He sighed. "Listen, I've got to go. I still have to talk to the police, I just thought that you should hear about all of this from me instead of from the news or from one of your friends. I wanted to tell you myself that I'm fine."

"Thank you," she said. "I'm going to go tell Candice

what happened. David, will you do me a favor? Don't go anywhere alone with Lenny, all right?"

"I won't." His tone hardened. "I'm going to tell the police everything that you and I talked about, then I'm going to come straight home."

CHAPTER TEN

Moira stayed up long after Candice went to bed that night. Even though she knew that David was uninjured, she couldn't help but worry about him. It terrified her that this most recent murder had happened only minutes before he had arrived at the bar. If he had been even a couple of minutes early, he might have been the victim himself. She hadn't felt safe since the first shooting had happened, and felt even more terrified now that three people had died.

This person is a serial killer, she thought. *He's not going to stop at three people. There's a very real chance that my husband could be next.* With that chilling thought, she poured herself another cup of coffee, and settled down on the couch to wait for David to come home.

She was jolted awake a while later by the dogs barking. Despite the caffeine, she had fallen asleep. She pulled back the curtain and looked out the living room window. Recognizing David's headlights, she pushed the throw off of her lap and stood up. Moments later, David was at the door and she was hugging him, thankful that he was home at last.

"I'm surprised you're still up," he said. "I thought you'd be in bed by now."

"I was too worried," she said.

"Why? I told you I was fine. I didn't want you to be anxious about anything."

"I know," she said, sighed. "It's just, so much has been happening. I guess I needed to see you for myself. I'm so terrified that you're going to be the killer's next target, David."

"Hey, it will get solved. The police are going over the evidence from the bar. There are security cameras in the parking lot, so they'll be able to identify everyone who went into the bar before the shooting. This is going to be over soon."

"Did they arrest Lenny?"

To her disappointment, David shook his head. "I spoke with Detective Jefferson privately, but the fact remains that we have zero physical evidence, and zero motive. Without so much as a witness, there isn't much that they can do besides ask him questions — which they've already done, of course."

"I don't understand, how could someone have gotten shot in a bar full of people, and no one saw who did it?"

. . .

"I don't know," he said. "It must have just happened too quickly. There were a lot of people there — it's a Saturday night, after all. If the shooter was discreet, he might not have been noticed in the chaos that followed."

Moira shook her head. "I just can't believe that. How could someone walk into a building that was full of people, shoot someone, and leave without getting caught?"

"I don't know," David said. "But, I'm going to be working with the bar's owner to find out. He gave me access to the security tapes too, just in case I can pick up on something that the police missed."

"Have you looked at them yet?"

He shook his head. "I haven't had a chance. I supposed I could take a look before bed. I'm too wired to sleep right now anyway."

. . .

"Can I look at them with you?" she asked. "You know I like being involved in your cases, and this one feels so personal."

"Sure," he said. "Are there leftovers? I'm going to go grab something to eat, then let's meet on the couch."

A few minutes later, Moira was back on the couch with the throw over her legs and another cup of coffee in her hands while David was bent over an ancient VCR by the television. "You know, when you said security tapes, I didn't think you actually meant... tapes."

"It's an old security system," he said. "Part of what took me so long was waiting for the copies to be made. I just hope this thing still works." He smacked the top of the VCR, and all of a sudden it came to life. Moira waited while he found the right input channel on the television, then he pressed play and joined her on the couch.

.   .   .

"All right," he said. "Watch carefully for Lenny. You remember when I told you how to tell if someone is carrying a handgun?"

"I do, though I doubt I'll be very good at it."

She leaned against David, watching the security footage play out in front of her. She tried to stay focused, but watching cars and people come and go wasn't the most enthralling thing, and soon she found her eyelids drooping.

When her husband jolted to his feet, she sat up with a start. "What is it?"

"I saw Lenny. Hold on, I've got to rewind this. I wish it had a remote control."

Back on the floor, he fiddled with the VCR, staring up at the television as he rewound the tape and paused it. Moira squinted at the image, but it was fuzzy. She certainly wouldn't have recognized Lenny from that image alone.

"Are you sure it's him?"

"I'm sure. He was wearing that coat when I saw him there this evening."

Moira frowned at the image. From above, Lenny's balding head was even more evident. The tape had caught him mid-stride, and she could see that his pants were just a hair too short. He certainly didn't look like someone who could kill three people in cold blood over the course of a week without getting caught.

"Hold on," she said suddenly. "Do you see that car, there?" She pointed at the screen. David frowned.

"I think so. Why? What stands out about it to you?"

·   ·   ·

"That decal on the back... can you zoom in?"

Her husband turned to look at her, one eyebrow arched. "I'm working with a thirty-year-old VCR player without a remote control. We're low tech tonight."

I've been spoiled by technology, she thought. With a sigh, she got off the couch and knelt on the floor in front of the television. "This car right here. I think that decal is the same one we saw on Wyatt's car. Remember, the paw prints?"

"I do." He frowned.

"Well, did you see him inside? He kind of stands out."

"Remember, the shooting had already happened by the time I got there. Everything was chaotic. I don't remember seeing him, but that doesn't mean anything."

"Poor guy. I hope he didn't witness it. He seems so nice. I told you how well Maverick and Keeva did at doggy daycare, didn't I?"

David nodded, but she could tell that he wasn't paying attention. He was still staring at the car.

"What is it?" she asked.

"When did Wyatt get to town?"

"Um, last weekend, I think. That's when they started moving everything in, at least. Why?"

"The first murder happened Monday," he said.

. . .

"So?"

"He drives a dark car. It's dark green, but could easily be mistaken for black."

"You don't think he did this, do you?"

"I don't know. Probably not. But I think I'm going to check him out. I don't remember seeing the police interview him, and like you said, he stands out. In the chaos, it's possible that the shooter left before the police got there."

"Well, fast forward the tape and see when the car leaves," Moira suggested.

He pressed a button on the VCR, and the two of them sat back on their heels to watch as the video raced forward. David pressed play when they saw a figure bend over the car's door. The person's face was in shadows, and Moira couldn't tell who it was as they opened the car door and got in, but judging by the speed that they pulled out of the parking lot, whoever it was was in a hurry. David paused the video.

"Look at the time stamp," he said. "This is about two minutes after the shots were fired."

CHAPTER ELEVEN

Moira was exhausted in the morning. Between watching the security footage with David and tossing and turning while she wondered who the killer was, she had gotten only a few hours of sleep at most. When she heard the sound of someone up and walking around downstairs in the morning, she knew that Candice was up, and gave up on getting back to sleep. She slipped out of bed, careful not to disturb David, and went downstairs with the dogs, who were thrilled to find that Candice was still there. After their happy greeting session, she let the dogs out back, and turned to face her daughter, who was holding a mug of freshly brewed coffee out to her.

. . .

"You look tired. How late did David get home last night?"

"Late," Moira said. She sipped the bitter black coffee and winced, but could already feel it waking her up.

"Did the police figure out who shot that man at the bar?"

"No." Realizing that she was giving her daughter one-word answers, she expanded. "David's got a couple of suspects, though."

"Do you have any ideas about who the killer is?"

Moira hesitated. She remembered the fuzzy image that she had seen on their television the night before. Even after seeing that, she still wasn't convinced that Wyatt had been there. They didn't even know for sure that it was his car. The decal was fuzzy; it could have been anyone who had a vehicle with a sticker in the same place. Somehow, it didn't feel right to mention Lenny either. David had been so adamant that it wasn't him. If he ended up being innocent, she didn't want to be the one who had started spreading rumors about him.

"I don't know," she said after a moment's hesitation. "There's a couple of people I have suspicions about, but nothing concrete."

"Well, I'm glad David got home okay and stuff. That was scary."

That was something that Moira could wholeheartedly agree with. The two of them continued to chat over breakfast, then David came downstairs, looking only marginally more rested than Moira felt.

"Good morning," he said. "Sorry for missing dinner last night, Candice. Did your drive go okay?"

. . .

"It wasn't too bad," she said. "Are you still coming to visit Reggie with us today?"

"I'm planning on joining you guys for lunch. I want to stop at the office first. I've got to look into a couple of things. Will you two be all right?"

"We'll be fine," Moira assured him. "We can stop at the farmhouse first, if that works for you, Candice. Then you can get your arrangements with Thelma out of the way, and you'll be able to relax for the rest of the day."

"Sounds good."

The drive out to the farmhouse was a familiar one. Candice had only lived there for a short time before disaster had befallen her and Eli, and the two of them had left the area while Eli recuperated from his injuries, but David had been running the microbrewery off of the property for much longer. Even though the house was currently being rented to Allison's aunt, Moira couldn't help but envision her future grandchildren playing on the porch as they pulled up. She knew that her persistent wish for Candice to move back to Maple Creek might never come true, but she still hoped that her vision would come true. She enjoyed having her family around her, and knew that she had taken it for granted far too often.

"I miss this place," her daughter said as Moira pulled onto the grass and shut off the engine. "I know it's silly, and that we didn't even live here for that long, but I really do miss it. I can't wait until they start rebuilding the candy shop this spring."

"You're going to reopen it?" the deli owner asked, feeling her heart lift.

"I mean, I plan to one day. I don't know when though. It's not just the physical rebuilding — I've got to pretty much come up with a whole new business plan, replace the stuff I lost, and try to figure out if it can really be successful long term. I kind of rushed through a lot of that when I opened it the first time."

"Let me know if you need any help," Moira said. "You know that I'm more than happy to go over everything you need with you."

The hopeful feeling didn't go away as the two of them walked up the stone pathway to the house. It helped push thoughts of the multiple murders out of her mind for the time being, for which she was grateful. The past week had been so focused on death. She wanted to be looking forward to the future, not living in constant fear of what it might bring her.

"Hey," Thelma called out cheerfully as she opened the door. "Come on in. I've got some tea if you'd like some, and we can go over that lease."

Moira smiled as she followed her daughter into the house that would hopefully be a family home again sooner rather than later. *David and the police will solve the murders*, she told herself. *I have other things to focus on. More important things, because what's more important than family?*

"That went well," Candice said an hour later when they were on their way back to town. "This whole landlord thing is easy. We got done talking way earlier than I expected."

"Wait until the pipes freeze, or the roof starts leaking," Moira said, smiling. "Then it won't be so easy anymore. I'm glad everything went smoothly, though. Thelma's a good woman."

"Yes, she is. It's weird, I keep thinking of her like my aunt because she's related to Allison, but I guess she isn't really. She's still nice, though, and I'm glad that she's the one who ended up renting the house. I don't know if I'd be able to trust it with a complete stranger."

·   ·   ·

"I'm glad too," Moira said. She turned onto Maple Creek's main street. "You sure you want to stop at the deli instead of going home?"

"I am," her daughter said. "I want to say hi to Allison, and plus... I miss the place. I used to spend a lot of time there, I feel like I should at least visit."

"Okay. We've got about an hour before we've got to meet David and Reggie, so whatever you want to do, we can do it."

The truth was, she didn't want to be so close to Perfect Paws until she heard back from David. He had said that he was going to run a background check on Wyatt, which would at least tell her whether or not he had a criminal record. She kept going over the security tape video in her mind. She had been so certain it had been his car the night before, but now, in the daylight, she was doubting herself.

. . .

Watching Candice and Allison reunite was enough to make her forget about her concerns temporarily. She was happy for them, especially now that both seemed to have come to terms with the discovery that they shared a father. Allison had worked for her for years, and the two girls had been fast friends long before they had found out that they were related. Knowing what she knew now, it was impossible to miss the fact that they were sisters.

"I'm glad you came to visit," Allison said. "I miss hanging out with you."

"I'll try to stop by more often," Candice promised. "I miss you, and my mom and David, of course. It's weird, I haven't even been gone for that long, and stuff seems to have changed. Is that a new store next door?"

"That's Perfect Paws," Allison said. "You should go check it out. I haven't had a chance yet, but one of the employees, Penny, came in the other day and said that we were welcome to stop by and get a tour.

I guess they're just about ready for their grand opening and want opinions."

"Have you seen it, Mom?"

"I have. I actually took the dogs there a couple of days ago. They're going to start going to doggy daycare there while I'm working."

"That's awesome," Candice said. She linked arms with her sister. "Let's go check it out together, Allison. I want to see what it's like before I go."

"I've got a break coming up..." Allison looked over at Moira, biting her lip. "Is it all right if I go with her, Ms. D.?"

Moira hesitated. Wyatt had possibly been at the bar the night before, and might even be a suspect in the murder. However, without any actual evidence, she didn't want to sully his name in front of her daughter and employee. It wouldn't be fair to spread false information about him if she was wrong, especially not when she would be working in the building next to his for the foreseeable future. She knew she couldn't just let her daughter go over there alone, though, so she decided that there was only one course of action.

"Sure," she said. "I'll go with you. I'm eager to see what they've done with the place since I last saw it."

CHAPTER TWELVE

Moira followed the two young women out of the deli and across the snowy meridian that separated the buildings. She already knew that Candice was going to love the pet shop. It was the sort of place that her daughter might have liked to work at when she was younger. She was sure Wyatt would have no trouble finding employees when the time came for him to expand and, judging from the interest in the Perfect Paws business cards that people had been taking from beside the register all week, he wouldn't have any shortage of customers either.

Just as Moira was about to follow her daughter inside, her phone rang. It was David, and she knew that she had to answer it. If he had some news relevant to the case, then she wanted to hear it right away.

"Go on," she said to the girls. "I'll be right behind you."

She leaned against the wall outside of the building and took David's call. He hardly waited for her to say hello before speaking.

"I solved the case," he said. "I'm on my way to the police station right now."

"You did?" She breathed out a slow sigh of relief. "How do you know? Who was it?"

"It was Wyatt," he said. She felt her blood run cold. She opened her mouth, but her voice caught in her throat. David kept talking. "I ran a background check on him. He'd never been convicted of any crimes himself, but he was involved in a case years ago, back when he would have been in high school, that included the arrest of three young men. Guess which three?" He waited for a moment, but when she didn't jump in with an answer, he continued. "The ones that were murdered. And get this, the guys were arrested on assault charges. From what I found out about the charges, it sounds like they jumped him and beat him up badly enough that he lost an eye. The murders didn't start until he came back to town. He definitely has motive, and I can place his car at at least one of the crime scenes. I can't believe it, but we did it, Moira. We caught the killer."

"David..." she managed to say. "Candice is in the store now. I've got to go."

She hung up, feeling as if ice were creeping through her veins. *There's no way that Wyatt can know that we know*, she thought. *I just have to go in there and get Candice out, without him noticing that something's off.* Forcing a smile, she walked through the front door, hoping that her daughter would be easy to find.

. . .

She found herself in a transformed entrance room. While the last time she had been there, the basic fixtures of the room had been installed, there hadn't been much more in it than a front desk. There were racks set up along the walls, laden with dog and cat food, toys, collars, and leashes. There was a brand-new computer on the front desk, along with a potted plant and a service bell. There was a display case off to the side, and though it was empty at the moment, she guessed that was where the dog cookies would be displayed.

Moira shook herself, stunned by the changes, but refocusing quickly on the task at hand. Candice was in here somewhere, possibly with a killer. It wasn't a pleasant thought, but the deli owner forced herself to breathe slowly and *think*. Acting rashly would only serve to make things worse. She couldn't afford to give Wyatt even the slightest hint that they were on to him.

"Hello?" she called out softly. She heard a laugh

from somewhere beyond the door that led to the daycare area, but didn't see anyone in that room when she looked through the interior window. Not comfortable with the idea of wandering around the building on her own, she approached the desk and hit the bell for service.

"I was just coming out." The voice behind her made her jump. Sure enough, it was Wyatt. His eye patch lent him an air of intimidation, even though the rest of his face was as kind as ever.

"S-sorry," she stammered, taking a half-step backward. "I was just looking for my daughter. She came in with one of my employees to see about a tour, but something came up and we need to go."

"Of course. Is everything okay?"

"Um, yes," she said. "It's fine. It's not an emergency or anything, we're meeting some people for lunch, and it got moved up." In all truth, their lunch meeting with Reggie would probably be delayed, at least if they wanted David to come. Once he told the police what he had found out, she had no doubts that he would want to stick around to see the outcome.

"I'm glad it's nothing important. You looked worried. I'm actually taking an important call in my office, but I think Penny took them into the grooming area. Feel free to go get them."

He gave her a tense smile and raised a hand in a half wave before walking away. Moira watched him go, her suspicions suddenly rising up, and her worry for her daughter getting pushed to the side. Candice wasn't anywhere near Wyatt, and Moira had no doubt that she would be safe with Penny and Allison. Wyatt, however, had already vanished to go and finish his important phone call, and she couldn't help but wonder what it was about. *I wonder if he knows that they're onto him*, she thought. What if he was making plans to flee the state? Or what if he was planning to kill someone else, and the police didn't arrive in time to stop it? Torn, she glanced behind her at the door that she knew would lead her to the grooming area. She still wanted to get her daughter safe, but the urge to figure out exactly what Wyatt was doing was equally strong... and Candice was on the far side of the building. That had to count as safe, for now, at least... right?

Moira inhaled slowly, glancing behind her one last time. She told herself that Candice *was* safe, and that she had a responsibility to make sure Wyatt didn't escape and hurt someone else. All she would do is listen in on his phone call, and keep her eyes on him until the police arrived. She would be careful, and she figured if he caught her down the staff hallway, she could make up some story about looking for the bathroom. *I'll just be careful*, she thought as she reached for the door handle.

She had never been in this part of the building before, and now she wished that she hadn't turned Penny down when the young woman had offered her a tour of it. The hallway was dark, and empty boxes and half used paint cans lined the walls, reminding her that the interior still wasn't completely finished. She heard the murmur of a voice coming from the far end of the hall, and began to move carefully in that direction.

She slipped past the half-open door to a dark room, her heart beginning to pound. Her main concern when she had come into Perfect Paws had been Candice, and then once she realized her daughter wasn't near Wyatt, it had been the worry that he might escape, or attack someone else before he was arrested. Now, however, she began to fear for herself. She was alone in a dark hallway, and at the end of it was a man who had killed three people in the past week, seemingly without batting an eye.

Just figure out who he's talking to, at least, she told herself. *You know you'll never forgive yourself if after all of this he escapes.* She continued to inch down the hallway, careful not to bump into any of the debris. Once, she froze, imagining that she heard the slow creak of a door opening, but when she turned to look, the door that she had come in from remained shut. She breathed out a sigh of relief and hurried the rest of the way toward the room the voice was coming from as quickly as she dared.

When she reached the door, she tried to peer through the frosted window, but with no luck. Wyatt's voice on the other side was muffled, but she thought he sounded agitated. *I need to hear more*, she thought. The door was an old one, with a large keyhole that looked promising. She bent down slowly, and tried to peer through it, but it didn't work anywhere near as well as it did in the movies. Instead, she tried pressing her ear to it, and sure enough, she could just make out what Wyatt was saying.

"I'm afraid he's going to get into trouble again. He's up to something, and I don't like it. Either talk to him yourself, or I will."

Wyatt fell silent, listening to whoever was on the other end of the line speak, and Moira puzzled over what she had heard. He didn't sound like a man who was planning an escape, but there was definitely an urgency to his voice that made her think that what-ever he was talking about was important.

"What are you doing back here?"

The whispered voice and a warm breath on her neck made her jump. The only thing stopping her from screaming was the hand that suddenly pressed over her mouth. She managed to half spin around, and found herself with her back pressed against the wall with her heart pounding, staring at Andre.

CHAPTER THIRTEEN

"What are you doing?" he repeated, his voice so soft she could hardly hear it. He held a finger to his lips, then slowly removed his hand from her mouth.

"Your uncle," she whispered back. "He's... he's the shooter."

Andre's eyes widened. "What are you talking about?"

"I know it's hard to believe, but his car was spotted at the bar last night. He was there when that man died. My husband — he's a private investigator — he ran a background check on him, and discovered that Wyatt knows all three of the men who were killed." She hesitated, then added, "They're the ones who caused him to lose his eye. I think he's getting revenge."

The young man was shaking his head, his expression shocked. "No, he didn't kill them."

"I know it's not what you want to hear, but you have to believe me," she whispered. "It's true. The police will be here any minute to arrest him."

Andre stood up suddenly, pulling her with him with an iron-like grip on her upper arm. She saw him reach into his pocket, then he spun her around, so she was facing the door again. She felt something razor edged and cold prick her neck. Her heart stuttered. What was going on? Was Andre so devoted to his uncle that he would kill her in an effort to keep the man's murderous secret?

. . .

"Don't make a sound," he breathed in her ear.

He turned her around and began to march her down the hallway. Moira didn't know where they were going, or what he was going to do with her, and she never found out because at that moment, the door at the other end of the hall opened and Penny stepped through. The three of them were frozen for the handful of seconds it took her to realize what she was seeing, then she screamed. Behind them, Wyatt's office door crashed open. Andre jerked around, slamming his back to the wall and holding Moira in front of him like a shield. The movement made the knife bite into her skin, and she gasped.

"Andre, what are you doing?" Wyatt snapped.

She felt Andre take a breath, but before he could reply, she heard from the other end of the hallway, "Mom!"

Moira turned her head as much as she could, and

saw her daughter standing next to Penny. Allison crowded in beside her, a horrified look on her face.

"Andre!"

The young man jumped, and Moira felt a drop of blood slide down her throat. "Sorry, Uncle Wyatt," he said. "I didn't plan on this, it just sort of happened."

"Let her go. What on earth are you doing?"

"I need a hostage," Andre said. "I'm getting out of here before the police get here."

"The police?" Wyatt sounded baffled. "What's going on? Get the knife away from her throat."

She felt, rather than saw, Andre shake his head behind her. "She's my safety net. I can't let her go. I'm sorry for bringing all of this back on Perfect Paws, Uncle. I didn't mean to get you in trouble."

Moira looked toward the other end of the hallway again, but Candice was gone. She felt her heart rise. She knew that her daughter hadn't abandoned her; no, she was prepared to bet her life that Candice was getting help.

"Andre, look, just put the knife down, and then we'll talk," Wyatt said in a soothing voice. "That's all — we'll just talk. I just want to know what's going on, because I'm completely lost here."

"I thought killing them would help," Andre said. He shifted, focusing more on his uncle now, and ignoring the girls at the other end of the hallway. "Those guys that beat you up? After you told me that story, I did some digging and found out who they were. They had to pay. You're living your entire life disfigured, and they got off with just a bit of jail time? It wasn't right. I made it right."

· · ·

Moira's mind focused on Andre's words, maybe because she was too terrified to focus on the knife at her throat. Andre was the killer, not Wyatt? He must have borrowed his uncle's car, she thought. We never actually saw Wyatt's face in the video.

"You... you did what?" Wyatt took a step backwards, a look of horror dawning on his face. "You killed those men?"

"I thought it would make you happy," Andre said. He had finally eased the pressure on the knife. It was still held to her throat, but she could no longer feel it biting into her skin. "You must have hated them. After everything you did for me — taking me in when my father kicked me out, helping me get off of drugs and away from that life — I wanted to do something for you too. What better way than killing the men who disfigured you?"

"They had families," Wyatt said, staring at his nephew as if seeing a stranger. "Wives, children... they were kids when they jumped me back in high school, and they shouldn't have attacked me, but me losing the eye was an accident. I tripped and fell, and they panicked and ran. That was over fifteen years ago. How could you ever think that this was something I wanted?"

"But, Uncle... we're family. You've always been more of a dad to me than my real dad. We stick together. That's what we do."

"Not after this," Wyatt said. "Let Moira go now. If you ever want me to speak to you again, let her go and put the knife down."

To her surprise, he did. Moira put a hand to her throat, and her fingers came away red with blood. She hurried down the hallway without looking back, half stumbling over the empty moving boxes. Penny and Allison reached out for her as she neared them, and she nearly ran headlong into Candice.

"Mom!" Her daughter wrapped her in a tight hug. "I

called the police and they're on their way. Are you okay? You're bleeding."

"I'm okay," she said. "It's just a scratch. That was a bit too close for comfort, though."

"I can't believe it," Penny said. "Andre killed all those people? I've been working alongside him every day."

She had a horrified look on her face, and Moira didn't blame her. She spared one last glance down the hallway, where Andre had slid to the floor and had his hands over his face. She could see his shoulders shaking. With a shiver, she turned away. As far as she was concerned, anyone who could murder three people in cold blood, and show up at work the day after without showing even a twinge of discomfort was someone who should have been behind bars a long time ago.

EPILOGUE

"Are you sure you want to be out?" David asked.

Moira sighed. Ever since the attack at Perfect Paws, her husband had been treating her as if she was made of glass. She hadn't minded at first, but by the third day, it was getting a bit wearing.

"I'm sure. This is Valentine's Day, and I want to celebrate it with you."

"Okay." He took her hand gently. "If that's what you want. Is your neck okay?"

. . .

"Seriously, David, it was just a scratch. I didn't even need stitches, remember? And I got a tetanus shot and antibiotics just in case." She readjusted her scarf. The cut may not have been much more than a scratch, but she was still self-conscious about it. The story about what had happened had, of course, somehow gotten out, and she didn't like the way that people stared at her. That didn't mean that she was going to stay home, though; she would have been ashamed of herself if she had let some stares and sideways looks stop her from enjoying Valentine's Day with her husband.

"Your table's ready."

She and David followed the hostess to their usual booth. It seemed as if everything in the restaurant had been replaced with something holiday themed. Even the cloth napkins were pink with embroidered hearts along the edges.

. . .

"Denise really goes all out, doesn't she," Moira murmured.

David chuckled. "She does. And the food is good, so I can't complain. Look over there." The last sentence he said more quietly, and inclined his head toward the other side of the room. Moira glanced in the direction he had indicated and raised her eyebrows. Cameron and Jenny were sitting at a small table, both of them looking very dressed up, and very nervous.

"I knew it," Moira whispered. "He's going to propose."

She tried not to stare at the couple, but it was difficult. She didn't want to miss the special moment.

"Are you sure you're okay?" David asked, for what she felt was the millionth time.

. . .

141

"I'm fine," she said. "I promise. I'm just glad we caught the right guy."

"I feel terrible for Wyatt," David said. "I think Andre was like a son to him. He stopped by the station to pick up some of Andre's things after we transferred him, and I could tell he was having a rough time of it."

"I'm sure it will be a long time before he comes to terms with what happened," Moira said. "I can't even imagine what it would be like if Candice did something like that, because I know that she never would. It must be the worst feeling in the world."

"I'm sure there were warning signs with Andre," David said. "Wyatt probably just didn't want to see them. The guy had a record a mile long, and he was only nineteen. He had an assault charge, a handful of drug charges, and was affiliated with some pretty bad people when he was still in high school. I think one of the reasons Wyatt moved them up here was to get Andre away from all of that."

. . .

"I just wish that none of this had happened," she said. "It's horrible to imagine what the families of those men must be going through."

"I know," he said, covering her hand with his. "It's terrible, there's no doubt about that. But not everything's wrong with the world. Look."

Moira did, just in time to see Cameron get down on one knee beside the table that he and Jenny were sitting at. Jenny leapt to her feet and was nodding before Cameron's lips began to move. By now, everyone in the restaurant was watching them, and when Jenny accepted the ring, applause burst out. Despite the horrors of the past week, the deli owner smiled. Terrible things would always happen, but she knew that at the same time, love would find a way to persevere.

ALSO BY PATTI BENNING

Papa Pacelli's Series

Book 1: Pall Bearers and Pepperoni

Book 2: Bacon Cheddar Murder

Book 3: Very Veggie Murder

Book 4: Italian Wedding Murder

Book 5: Smoked Gouda Murder

Book 6: Gourmet Holiday Murder

Book 7: Four Cheese Murder

Book 8: Hand Tossed Murder

Book 9: Exotic Pizza Murder

Book 10: Fiesta Pizza Murder

Book 11: Garlic Artichoke Murder

Book 12: On the Wings of Murder

Book 13: Mozzarella and Murder

Book 14: A Thin Crust of Murder

Darling Deli Series

Cozy Mystery Tails of Alaska

Book 1: Mushing is Murder

Book 2: Murder Befalls Us

Book 3: Stage Fright and Murder

Book 4: Routine Murder

Book 5: Best Friends and Betrayal

Book 6: Tick Tock and Treachery

AUTHOR'S NOTE

I'd love to hear your thoughts on my books, the storylines, and anything else that you'd like to comment on—reader feedback is very important to me. My contact information, along with some other helpful links, is listed on the next page. If you'd like to be on my list of "folks to contact" with updates, release and sales notifications, etc.... just shoot me an email and let me know. Thanks for reading!

Also...

... if you're looking for more great reads, Summer Prescott Books publishes several popular series by outstanding Cozy Mystery authors.

CONTACT SUMMER PRESCOTT BOOKS PUBLISHING

Twitter: @summerprescott1

Bookbub: https://www.bookbub.com/authors/summer-prescott

Blog and Book Catalog: http://summerprescottbooks.com

Email: summer.prescott.cozies@gmail.com

YouTube: https://www.youtube.com/channel/UCngKNUkDdWuQ5k7-Vkfrp6A

And...be sure to check out the Summer Prescott Cozy Mysteries fan page and Summer Prescott

Books Publishing Page on Facebook – let's be friends!

To download a free book, and sign up for our fun and exciting newsletter, which will give you opportunities to win prizes and swag, enter contests, and be the first to know about New Releases, click here: http://summerprescottbooks.com

Made in the USA
Coppell, TX
23 May 2021